Rita and the
Flying Saucer

Also by Hilda Offen:

Rita on the River

Rita Rides Again

Rita and the Romans

RITA THE RESCUER

Rita and the Flying Saucer

Hilda Offen

troika books

For Alice

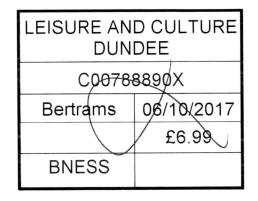

Published by TROIKA BOOKS

First published 2017

1 3 5 7 9 10 8 6 4 2

Text and illustrations copyright © Hilda Offen 2017

The moral rights of the author/illustrator have been asserted

A CIP catalogue record for this book
is available from the British Library

ISBN 978-1-909991-56-9

Printed in Poland

Troika Books
Well House, Green Lane, Ardleigh CO7 7PD, UK

www.troikabooks.com

"Look at those lights!" said Eddie. "What do you think they are?"

"Shooting stars!" said Julie.

"Lightning!" said Jim.

"Perhaps it's a spaceship," said Rita.

"RITA! DON'T BE SILLY!" they shouted.

The next day Eddie, Julie and Jim jumped on their skateboards.

"We're going to investigate," said Eddie. "We think a spaceship landed last night."

"I said that!" said Rita. "Can I come?"

"No, you can't," said Julie. "Why don't you stay in and watch the Tubbly-Bubblies?"

Rita stamped indoors and switched on the television. The screen flickered and a strange face appeared. It said, "Greetings from the Planet Norma Alpha."

"Ho-hum!" said Rita. "More work for the Rescuer."

And she changed into her outfit and whizzed out of the window.

Outside in the street some Norms were approaching a litter-bin.

"Can I help?" asked Rita.

"No!" they said. "Go away. You're much too small."

"Please yourselves!" said Rita and she moved so quickly the Norms were left blinking.

"Hallo!" said Rita as she flew over the allotments. "I spy trouble."

A Norm was trying to steal Mr McGregor's prize marrow.

"DROP THAT MARROW!"

Rita's roar was so fierce that Mr McGregor
and the Norm fell backwards.

Mr McGregor landed in a bed of marigolds
but the Norm fell into the compost heap.

"Ugh!" he said. "I'm off!" and he
scrambled out and flew away
into the distance.

"You've got an amazing roar, Rescuer!"
said Mr McGregor.

"Thank you!" said Rita. "Uh-oh! I'm needed
at the supermarket."

"Bring back my cornflakes!"
yelled Mr Biggins.

"They've got our skateboards!"
screamed Julie and Jim.

Rita ran like an antelope. She leaped on the back of the skateboards and the Norms shot in the air.

"Now hand over those cornflakes!" said Rita.

"Not likely!" said the Norms and they raised their deadly jelly guns.

"Boing!" The jelly bounced off Rita's chest and shot back at the Norms. "Splat!" They were covered from head to toe.

"Help!" cried little Lucy Gill as the Norms squelched away. "There's some more of them! They've got Tigger, my hamster!"

Oh no! The Norms weren't looking where they were going. They were heading straight for a helicopter!

Rita didn't hesitate. She zoomed
after the jet-scooter, seized the controls
and steered it out of harm's way.

"Look where you're going in future," she
said. "That could have been very nasty."

Then she grabbed Tigger and took him back
to Lucy; but she had no time for a breather.

"Rescuer!" screamed a little boy. "There's an alien in the playground. He's going round and round on the swings!"

Sure enough, there on a swing was a little Norm. His jet-pack had jammed and he was whizzing round like a windmill.

Rita caught the swing and hung on till it stopped. A plume of smoke rose in the air.

"Boo-hoo!" wept the little Norm. "It's too far to walk back to the flying saucer. I'm lost!"

"There, there!" said Rita. "Where did you leave the saucer?"

"Don't know!" sobbed the Norm. "There were tall posts with green stuff on top. And small furry beings with long ears."

"Hm!" said Rita. "Those sound like trees. And rabbits. I think you're talking about Foxley Wood. Come on!"

"We're too late!" cried the Norm as they reached the wood. "They're taking off!"

Quick— let's get out of here!

19

He was right! All the jet-scooters were returning to the flying saucer! Worse still, Eddie was in one of them.

"Help!" he screamed as the doors slammed shut.

Rita picked up an abandoned space-helmet.

'"Put this on!" she said. "We've no time to lose!"

They shot upwards and after
a while they saw the flying
saucer ahead of them.

Rita rapped on the window.

"Open the air-lock!" gasped
the captain.

Mum!

It's my
little Zark! I
wondered where
he was.

"Why have you kidnapped that boy?
And that cat? And that pig?" asked Rita.
"And what are you doing with those chips?"
  "We are running short of our special food,
the Googoo fruit," said the captain. "We had
hoped to survive on your earth food. But we
cannot eat it."

"And we're lost!" said his second-in-command. "We are trying to find a clever earthling who can guide us home."

"But it's hopeless!" said the captain. "So far they have scored nought out of ten."

"Test me!" said Rita; so they did.

"Ten out of ten!" cried the Norms. "What a brain!"

"Not even our wisest old Norm can find the way home on the star chart," said the captain. "Will you take a look?"

"With pleasure," said Rita. "Aha! An easy enough mistake. You were holding the map upside down. There's Norma Alpha."

"But it is a thousand light years away!" said the captain. "We only have enough Googoo fruit for a week."

24

"I know a short cut," said Rita. "There you are! That should only take you two or three days."

"Thank you, thank you, Rescuer!" cried the Norms as Rita and Eddie sped away in a jet-scooter, along with the cat and the pig.

Go carefully!

You can keep the jet-scooter.

"Nearly home!" said Rita.
"Oh no – more trouble!"
An asteroid was heading
for earth.

"POW!" Rita shattered it by flying at it with her head. It fell to earth in a shower of stardust.

Down on the Sports Field hordes of people had gathered. There were TV cameras and reporters amongst them.

Rita landed the jet-scooter and everyone cheered.

"They're all yours!" Rita said to the reporters. "I have to go!"

"Still watching TV, Rita?" asked Julie later on that night. "You'll get square eyes."

"You missed the Rescuer again!" cried Jim.

"I was abducted by aliens!" said Eddie. "The Rescuer saved me! And she saved the earth from being hit by an asteroid."

"I know!" said Rita. "I've seen it all on the News."

I wish I could be like the Rescuer, Mum.

Look out for other Rita titles from Troika Books

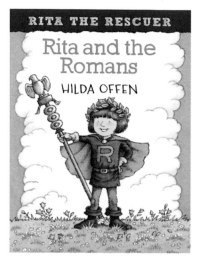

Rita and the Romans

There's plenty of work for Rita to do when it's
Roman day at the Sports Field – a toddler's being
launched in the air from a giant catapult, a trumpeter's
in trouble and there's Adrian's Wall to build.

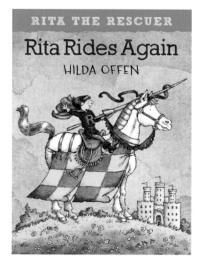

Rita Rides Again

Whether it's ghosts in the castle,
monsters in the moat or a flock
of angry peacocks, you can count
on the Rescuer!

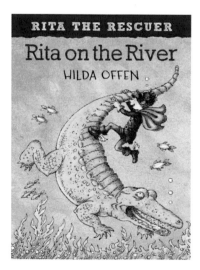

Rita on the River

Rita rescues a puppy that can't swim,
assists an island castaway and saves
some swimmers from a giant crocodile
about to open its fearsome jaws!